THE COMMONS

Part One

Bleu Olive

Bleu Olive

genishamorton.com

Printed in the United States of America

First Printing: Aug 2018

Genisha Morton

ISBN-978-0-578-88213-0

DEDICATION

I dedicate this story to Mrs. Tammie Terrell Polk, thank you for seeing me when all I wanted to do was disappear. Thank you for helping me to rewrite this story to its fullest capabilities without running from the truth. To my sons, my daily inspiration to be great. I appreciate you for loving me through all my flaws and imperfections. Kameron, thank you for teaching me to be confident and courageous, Kalaab, thank you for encouraging me to do it big and bold, Isaiah, thank you for daring me to be what I say.

CONTENTS

PREFACE

Family Secrets…

Where did they start and how deep do they go?

One thing that unites the world is a family full of secrets… and my dreams have told me the stories of three families who struggle with the aftereffects of many secrets that can no longer stay buried…

INTRODUCTION

Imani thought she could keep her life and her past hidden…
until…

One day, she runs into the one person who'd bring it all to the surface.

Times were changing and her family was struggling to make things happen.

Her family is moved into a housing program while her son investigates a woman who brings Imani's past into her present.

Foreword by Tammie Polk

Although this is a fictional book, it reminds us that there will always be someone who seeks to be in control! What I like about Genisha's story is that there is an overcomer who shows us that no matter what our family or foe does; we can overcome that control. In a way, this book speaks of the future—a woman who seeks to control her small corner of the world in an effort to control the ONE person she can't stand. I can't wait for you to see what happens! I am proud of Genisha because this was not an easy story for her to write. This book covers subjects that many battle with every day, yet they are ones that need not be swept under a rug. So, if you see yourself in the person of any character here, do so with the mindset that you too will overcome just as they did. Your past does not define you… What people do or have done to you does not define you… Rising above is possible… Rising above is real… It's time for YOU to RISE!!!

Tammie Polk

Author of 30+ books

#writingmywaythroughlife

CHAPTER ONE

A New Beginning

"I am Helen, your Commons guide. I will take you around the facility so you can see that all your needs are met in this one building.
—Helen White

"Welcome to the Commons. Here, we are more than a simple community, we are family! It is my pleasure to welcome you home. We know times are hard and keeping up with the changes can be quite overwhelming; therefore, I created this program for those of you who may have lost your previous lifestyles and those on government assistance who may have lost their help.

I am Helen, your Commons guide. I will take you around the facility so you can see that all your needs are met in this one building. Each of the compartments was built based on your submitted surveys. The tour will start in the next five minutes. If you have any questions, please ask your Team Lead. They will introduce themselves momentarily. Please listen for your name and go to the area where that Team Lead is standing. Again, welcome home and enjoy the view!"

Helen finished her speech better than she'd planned. Everyone believed in the allusion she created, and no one saw the smirk on her face as they began to walk around the facility. She walked back to her office, which she named BWIC, and began to work on her plan. She figured if she couldn't get into the White House because of her past, she'd build her own.

Helen was so caught up with her thoughts that she hardly noticed the elderly woman, who was not impressed. She didn't talk much but kept an eye on the things that Helen said and did. She joined the tour party late, yet she was able to catch up and noticed the Team Leads were doing a great job.

The families loved the convenience of everything, and the kids loved the playground and other kid areas. Helen smiled as she saw things coming together nicely and was confident that her plan was flawless. She'd been back in the office lost in planning and working on the computer when she noticed feet at her door. She nearly jumped out of her seat.

"I didn't see you," Helen regained her composure. She wondered how long he'd been standing there, and what he saw. Before she could give herself away, he began to speak.

"No luck," Bailey exclaimed.

"Then you shouldn't be standing here! You should be out there looking! Do NOT come back until you've found what I've sent you to find!" Bailey wanted to say more, but the look on Helen's face said that wasn't a good idea. Bailey headed out the door but turned to say something. At the last minute, he changed his mind.

"How do I tell her this girl is not interested? Who is she anyway?" Bailey made some contacts to help persuade this young lady to change her mind. As he began to call his private contacts, the desk phone rang.

"I hope you know your life is on the line. Don't cross me." Helen hung up the phone once she completed her demand. Bailey was growing tired of her pushing him around. He contacted his help and hoped this would work. He didn't want to go this far, but he felt he had no choice.

The world was changing at a rapid pace, and America wasn't the nation it used to be. It still had a strong lead yet declining more each decade. It seemed everyone had a scheme for a better life. It was hard to decipher between the real programs and the scams.

The government had plans set in motion to eliminate the welfare, housing, and healthcare programs to save money. Though nothing was set in stone, Helen was still able to use this to her advantage. The fear of loss caused many to move in without asking too many questions. The Commons appeared to be the place of hope and the new start they needed.

The "new America" didn't include the poor, so they had to figure it out on their own. The sound of their children's laughter was the reason many were able to relax and see a positive future.

While residents were asking questions that were not being answered, they didn't worry too much. It was still a new experience and they figured things would eventually come together.

They discovered Helen wasn't mistaken when she said everything they need was inside of the building. There were restaurants, grocery stores, doctor's offices, children's playgrounds, and restaurants, movie theaters—everything they could think of was at their fingertips.

Like every housing program, The Common had rules, but theirs were based on a point system. The points were equivalent to money and earned by completing chores and participating in community events, which the residents weren't too sure about. There were no specifics given and requirements seemed to change with Helen's mood swings.

Helen also made it mandatory for families to interact with one another. She hoped to get an earful of gossip that would keep her in the loop even when she wasn't there. Not following the rules led to consequences that ranged from losing privileges to being evicted. The residents wondered where they would go from there if that were to happen, so everyone stayed on their p's and q's.

"All Things in Common" was posted on all the compartments alongside their list of chores and some other dos and don'ts. The goal was for everyone to have everything in common. No more or no less than their neighbor, so that no two families would leave on the same day or in the same month. Helen wanted to maintain as much control as she could until she could legally have full control.

Her plan was coming along nicely, and her final piece was finding her high school rival, Jennifer Collins. She was determined to make her pay for high school and payback is a bitch. Bailey found her but couldn't convince her to move to The Commons or even look in his direction. Helen was excited to see that her long-lost foe was a recipient of Section 8 housing and she was more than happy to use it against her.

It was a muggy afternoon in February, and threats of snow had been announced. Jennifer is finally able to leave for school after nearly three hours of feeding, dressing, redressing the boys, and getting everyone to school and daycare. How do kids make the messes they do so quickly—she will never know. This routine became habitual because somehow, one of them would always tend to have an accident. "Oops" and "Uh-oh" were stated at least one hundred times a morning.

One day, Jennifer decided to give the boys a granola bar with the intent of them eating a full breakfast once they got to school. It was a brilliant idea until they still found a way to mess up their clothes and the baby had it all over his face and in his hair.

Since then, Jennifer plans so that everything runs more smoothly. Today seemed to be an off day.

No one wanted to get out of bed including Jennifer, everyone was a bit cranky, breakfast wasn't a smooth flow, and the weather wasn't that great. The cold weather seemed to make everyone drag their feet. Jennifer's priorities were taking care of her sons, working, and getting her degree. She had little time for distractions or anything else. The struggle was real, but her dream to become a psychiatrist wasn't far away.

She was finally the top student in her classes and able to put the horrors of high school behind her. She used the flashbacks as tools to push herself forward. She had to be available for the women who'd come after her. If she could help it, there was no way she'd let anyone go through what she went through.

As she walked to her car, she notices Bailey sitting on the curb and doesn't even look up to shout "NO!" She couldn't figure out what was so hard for him to understand about the word no. She sits in her car and notices some mail she forgot to take in the house from the weekend. One of the envelopes had "Urgent" written on it and she regretted she overlooked it.

"Oh boy what is it now?" Jennifer said to herself as she opened the letter. What she saw was devastating and made her feel as if all hope were lost. She steps out of the car, catching Bailey before he leaves. With tears in her eyes, she agrees to visit the place that he's been trying to get her to visit for almost six months now. Bailey sees the envelope and realizes his plan worked. He hated he had to do things the way he did, but he was desperate.

Bailey had monitored Jennifer for approximately six months and couldn't make heads or tails of Helen's accusations. Jennifer seemed to stay to herself and with her sons. There was never a moment where she interacted with other people. People he knew that were bullies usually made it their business to find their next victims. If she was such a horrible person, where was the horrible? Honestly, the only one he saw that was guilty of being a monster was Helen. They did bear a striking resemblance and he wondered if they were sisters.

Guilt struck, he returned to the office and pondered some more about his case. He had a lot of responsibility in front of him, and he wasn't sure how to handle it. On his desk was a picture he glanced at that helped him remember why he accepted this case in the first place.

"I'm going to find you, and I'm bringing you home." Bailey wiped the tears from his eyes and returned to his undercover character. Too much was at stake and he had to make sure everything was done correctly. They were going to catch her this time.

Helen's mood swings were unpredictable and confusing. Now Jennifer is no longer the enemy but the Golden Child. Helen was seen around the Commons celebrating her anticipated arrival. She shared stories with other residents about how her bestie from high school was coming and it's her honor for

Jennifer to be there. Bailey couldn't ignore prior complaints he'd received about Helen, but maybe she'd changed.

Jackson called Bailey to get an update on the case and got an earful of how Helen has gone from the Wicked Witch of the South to Suzie Homemaker.

"You should see this! It's a regular TV show. I have no idea what she's going to do next." Jackson laughed.

"Stay calm and don't blow your cover! I know this investigation came at a bad time for you. We are grateful for your sacrifice, but just be careful. She's gotten away with too much already." Bailey agreed.

"I know how important this is. I won't screw this up. Let me get back before she switches back over to the other lady." Bailey hung up the phone. He was fine until Jackson mentioned the fact that he was taken away from something more important. The promise to have full support for his project was enough to get him to join the team.

Jackson understood better than anyone else what Bailey was going through because he had the same situation himself. He just couldn't speak much about it until he got more information. Jackson slapped his hands together and said, "God, PLEASE help this man keep his cool! He can be a bit presumptuous sometimes."

Helen's temper was always explosive, yet she had hidden it for years. The closer it comes to Jennifer's move-in date, the more unstable her temper seemed to become. Even she was thrown off sometimes by her mood swings, she liked the results that came from it. It got her what she wanted why, so she didn't try and fix it.

"When are you going to pick up Jennifer or do I have to do everything myself?" Helen cornered Bailey in her office. The mean Helen was back, and he needed to have answers for her. He was growing tired of her but understood the bigger picture.

Jennifer was struggling with her move. The closer it came to her move date, the more her past haunted her in her dreams.

She was clueless as to why and shook it off so she could focus on what was in front of her.

"I'm going to see what the college has available on campus. I thought I didn't have to worry about that, but this is the last time I depend on the government to help me. I'm doing this myself. I don't have a good feeling about this place." Jennifer packed the remainder of her things and took a deep breath.

"This is messing up my timeline." Jennifer prepared to get the boys from school and promised them they wouldn't be there long. The Commons was too much like living in a shelter and Jennifer hated shelters. The unknown had too much uncertainty and Jennifer wasn't sure.

One sleepless night after another, her past haunted her and it was beyond her control. She decided to see someone about what she was going through. While Helen was preparing for Jennifer's arrival, she received an unexpected visitor.

"Mrs. White, one of the rules is that we mentor someone new to the Commons. I would like to get the next new intake. You've spoken quite well of her, so I thought she'd be a good fit for me." Helen turned to see who was speaking to her.

"It's Helen. You don't have to call me Mrs. White." She reached out to shake the elderly woman's hand, but the offer was rejected.

"Mrs. White, when she arrives, please have her meet me in my compartment. I'd like to get started as soon as possible. I'll have my son escort her so that she doesn't get lost." The elderly woman had a smirk on her face that made Helen squirm.

"By the way, what's your name?" Helen asked trying to make a connection.

"You will know when you know. Don't forget to tell Jennifer I'll meet with her when she gets here." Satisfied, the elderly woman returned to her compartment. Helen scratched her head wondering where if she knew the elderly woman from somewhere. A feeling in her stomach and some memories that flashed before her told her of a story she spent years trying to forget.

"Who is she?" Helen goes back to her office, making sure to cover her tracks. "What if she knows something? What I'm doing?" Helen was afraid and couldn't shake the mystery of who this elderly woman was.

"Bailey, bring me everything you have on that woman! Where are you?" Bailey sent the phone to voicemail. He was focused on his problems and didn't want to be disturbed. He knew if he answered the phone, he'd blow the case.

"Jackson, I've found some evidence I think you'd be interested in. Don't forget your promise to me." Bailey ended the text and started to make his way to the Commons.

"She always calls at the wrong time. When is this going to be over?" Bailey took a deep breath and made plans to stop for drinks before going home. It was the only way he knew of to keep his cool. He wasn't an alcoholic, but it came in handy on cases like this. "This woman is somethin' else." Bailey thought to himself as he drove into the complex. It took him ten minutes to get out of the car and walk into the building.

"Great, you got my messages." Helen hastily pushed Bailey into her office and closed the door. "That lady is crazy, and I want everything about her in my hands in the next 24 to 48 hours." Helen was pacing back and forth as she explained what she wanted Bailey to do.

"She's not the only one." Bailey thought as he set out to complete everything on Helen's list. "Is there anything else ma'am?" Bailey had to control the urge to roll his eyes and tell Helen what he thought of her.

"Protect the case." He repeated to himself to maintain control.

"For this community to work, we have to stick together. I want to weed out the bad so that all who remain are good." Helen explained as she escorted Bailey out.

* * *

"A Perfect World"

Several months had passed and things were flowing smoothly. Helen could see herself arriving at a point where she would be in full control. No one would ever control her again. The people who made her life miserable were finally going to see her shine. Helen banked on convenience.

"Why leave when everything you need is right here in front of you? They won't want to leave and when they do; it'll be too late." Helen chuckled to herself.

The elderly woman was a bit mysterious to the other residents. She seemed to have a way with Helen that kept her in line. Then again, it was her gimmick. She kept everyone in line so why would Helen be any different. She was the mother so many needed and, to others, the big sister or aunt—no matter what her role, she made the Commons feel like home.

Helen wanted to keep the money circulating within the Commons. She had the residents exchange their cash for what she called Common Dollars that would only work within their community. No one could purchase anything or go anywhere without a certain amount of Common Dollars in their account. This was Helen's way of stealing the residents' money without them being suspicious.

"This is my world with little minions who follow my every bidding, no… COMMAND sounds much better!" Helen laughed to herself. "It's finally my turn to be in control and nothing's gonna stop me." Helen gave her jacket a slight tug. "Now to deal with that old lady. I've got to get her out of here before she blows everything. *'Mrs. White?'* Who does she think she is? I will teach her to snoop around in other peoples' business." Unaware the elderly woman was standing by, she continued to plot aloud.

The elderly woman wasn't shocked by what she heard. She expected it and everything was right on schedule. Helen was most impressed with money and those who had the most had the best. She realized that she had the least control over them. Those who had the least had the worst and she had the most control over them. Her goal was to find a balance where she always had full control of all residents.

Some of the residents were uneasy about turning over all their money to Helen. They didn't trust how she did things, so they started saving to rebuild when they were able to. Some had been smart enough to not let her know how much they had, pretending to not have a lot. The rest didn't plan for a rainy day because they didn't expect the rainy days to drown them out as much as they did.

The elderly woman got under Helen's skin, but Helen managed to resist putting her out because she helped maintain peace and order. She knew that, with the elderly woman there, her rules would be followed exactly the way she wanted.

After six months, the honeymoon period was over, and it was time to up the ante. Curfews were a new addition to the growing list of rules. Life for those who opted to keep their kids in schools outside of the Commons was harder than they needed it to be. Point requirements increased yet amounted to nothing.

Helen had them right where she wanted them. The one good thing that did happen was that the residents became family.

Each would chip in to help the other without Helen noticing. They didn't want anything else taken away from them. She continually thought of ways to keep them down and all of them were illegal.

Family and Friends Day was the one event everyone was looked forward to. They did their best to stay on Helen's good side so she wouldn't take that away from them. Family and Friends Day happened once a month and was an open invitation for the residents to invite their family and friends for a visit. This way no one is homesick, and their families can see that they're living a lovely lifestyle. It was also Jennifer's move-in day.

What Helen didn't notice was that Jennifer had gotten the wrong information and moved in a month early, going unnoticed. She moved quietly and stayed in her compartment unless she was taking the boys to school or going to school or work herself.

She kept up her routine and didn't talk to anyone. Her goal was to be free from government assistance and was on her way to living in the family housing on campus. She was ready to be responsible for her own life and not depend on anyone or anything else other than God.

Jennifer wasn't expecting her family to show up. They never came to anything she invited them to anyway. She planned a fun day at home with her sons, and they were going to explore their new surroundings while everyone else was busy with their families. While she wondered why no one had been to her compartment to talk to or welcome her, she didn't care. She wasn't going to be there long and didn't want to be bothered. It was okay by her that it was just her and her boys—she'd grown accustomed to it.

Jennifer's family didn't treat her well. She was the literal black sheep of the family. Her skin was too dark, and she was too bald and ugly when she was born. She was an outsider from the beginning and there was nothing she could do but accept it.

When Jennifer became a mom none of that mattered to her and she wasn't raising her sons with that same hatred. She moved into a place where they could be themselves. Her Section 8 voucher allowed her to live on her own without having to depend on anyone.

This move came as a surprise and she hadn't been able to reach the Section 8 caseworker to find out what was going on. Thankfully, the door was still open for her to receive campus housing. Her internships guaranteed her a job once she graduated, so she wasn't worried. She couldn't shake the feeling that something was off but, for now, she was going to play it by ear.

"Hi, my Bears, how was your day?" It was one of the questions Jennifer would ask her sons daily. She had to be ready to get an earful and everyone got the same amount of time to share. If not, they'd all overtalk and outtalk each other, which sounded like a bunch of shouting and Jennifer wouldn't hear a word said.

The year was 2011 and something had to be different this year. Jennifer refused to be caught in the cycle of depending on government assistance forever.

It was the weekend and Jennifer wanted to keep her promise to make her Bears' big breakfast and watch their favorite cartoons.

She woke up before the boys and made all their favorites: pancakes, biscuits, bacon, cheese eggs, cheese grits, cinnamon rolls, orange juice, hot chocolate with marshmallows, and fruit. The boys were so excited to come to breakfast when they woke up! They enjoyed all of it and had the traditional dry cereal while they watched cartoons as well. How were they still hungry after eating all that? Only God knew.

They had a fun day as they explored the entire building. The kids loved the play area and the game room. Jennifer was happy to see them happy. Soon, the elderly woman spotted Jennifer returning to her compartment.

"Hello, I'm Imani. I have been waiting to meet you and would like a chance for us to talk."

CHAPTER TWO

Family and Friends Day

"I can't afford fun right now. Many choices were made for me..."—Jennifer Collins

Family and Friends Day was this weekend and Jennifer still hadn't heard anything from her caseworker. She paced back and forth in her living room while the phone rang.

"Why don't these people ever answer their phone or return a phone call?" Jennifer growled as she hung up her phone. She had a moment where she forgot if this was a workday or a school day but remembered it was Monday. School was on Mondays, Wednesdays, and Fridays. Work was on Tuesdays and Thursdays and the best part was they were all in the same location. Jennifer thought about getting a part-time job, but for now, school and her sons were her focus. Another job would interfere with her time with her boys.

"Nothing I can do about that until they call. Maybe Section 8 doesn't exist anymore. At least for me, it doesn't." Jennifer grabbed her keys and headed towards school. "Maybe, since I'm early, they'll let me get extra hours at work before I go to class." On her way out, she ran into Imani.

"Good Morning!" Imani greeted.

"Good Morning. I am on my way to class, and I will be able to talk this afternoon." Imani nodded to say she understood. Jennifer continued to her car wondering who that strange lady was.

"Nosy much?" Jennifer thought to herself.

"Hi Jen, you are just in time for a morning cap!" Laaek grabbed her bestie and dragged her to the cafeteria for breakfast.

"You're eating—my treat—cause while I know you cooked breakfast for my Godsons, you didn't eat yourself. My treat!" Jennifer picked out her breakfast and had a seat. She knew that, when her best friend was determined to do something, there was no stopping her. Plus, she knew her better than she knew herself sometimes.

"I know she has a camera on me somewhere. I've got to find it and destroy it." Jennifer mumbled to herself as she waited for her breakfast. "What's the news or whatever?" Jennifer asked.

"I have got a guy for you. You are going to love him!" Jennifer stopped her friend mid-sentence.

"What part of 'I'm not interested' don't you understand? I'm finishing school and raising my kids. That's it! I'm not saying this again." Laaek knew that, when Jennifer put her foot down, she meant it.

"I'm just lookin' out for you! You should have fun, too!" Jennifer fought back tears.

"I can't afford fun right now. Many choices were made for me, so now I'm handling those responsibilities and fun is on hold. In the meantime, I am having fun with my kids and completing my goal list. I'm going to get extra hours in at work. My first class isn't until 10 am, but I had to get away from that place. It's weird." Jennifer finished her breakfast and showed her tongue to prove she chewed and swallowed. She hugged her bestie and headed out the door with her juice in a to-go cup.

Laaek was concerned that she wasn't dealing with the issues of her past the way she needed to and didn't know how to get her to loosen up. She was afraid she was going to collapse under all the pressure, so she began working on another way to get her to relax and see a therapist. Jennifer was able to get a few extra hours at work, but suddenly, she didn't feel good and was dizzy.

"Are you okay, Jennifer?" A coworker noticed she was beginning to look pale, and her breathing was fast-paced. Alston helped her sit down.

"Yeah, I just got a little dizzy and nauseous, but I'm okay. I must have eaten too fast or somethin'." One of the doctors in the office gave her a checkup and determined she had a panic attack.

"This is the third time this month, Jennifer, and before you have a complete breakdown, we are recommending you to Dr. Tammie. T. Polk. She is expecting you to show up on Friday afternoons after your last class. This is non-negotiable. Now, I'm going to do you a favor, pay you for the hours you are not going to work, demand that you go to the lounge area, and take a nap, or a break, or whatever." Jennifer appreciated Dr. Harris because he was like the father she never had.

Jennifer was too tired to argue, so she obeyed. Frankly, her panic attacks were starting to scare her, too. For the next few days, Jennifer tries to contact the Section 8 office to no avail. She throws her hands up in frustration and decides it's hopeless. Nothing seemed to go right that day.

It was now Friday and her first meeting with Dr. Polk was a hard one. She didn't want to live in this place. The campus housing office told her it would be another month before they could get her in, and she wasn't very happy about that. From there, she made the day all about her boys, and movie night was on.

"We're having pizza, ice cream, popcorn, candy, and all the junk food we can handle! It's a Disney night and I'm glad about it!" Jennifer went to pick up her boys from after-care and off to the store they went.

"Are you okay, Mom?" Sean asked.

"Yeah, Mom, you don't look so good." Sam chimed in.

"Really? I feel good. I am looking forward to the movie night and all the junk food we're gonna eat. The pizza is coming, and we've got all these goodies. No interruptions—just us. I am good." Jennifer managed to cover up her real feelings when it came to her boys, even though she felt like they knew she was lying. They were too young to handle any of the stuff she was flustered about, so she dealt with it on her own. They got to their compartment and put away the groceries.

"Any homework, anyone?" The boys shook their heads no. "Okay! I have some, cause once you get to college, they don't care about weekends. I'm going to get started and do as much as I can before our movie night at 5 pm. Then, we are in for the night of our lives! You are free to play your video games after you have read one book." The boys were excited.

"Mom, are you sure everything is okay?" Sean couldn't shake the feeling that something was seriously wrong.

"I will be once I get a little of this work knocked out." Sean smiled and hugged his mom.

"Okay, don't worry, Mom. You'll do good!" Sean joined his brother and grabbed a book from their stash. They began to read to their little brother then help him with his letters and numbers. Jennifer loved that they stepped in to help him the way they did. She went to do her homework, and, to her surprise, she was able to complete a great deal of it before their movie time.

"It's time! Who's excited?" The boys all shouted "Me" as they headed towards the living room to sit on the floor and enjoy Disney movies.

"Someone's at the door," Sam heard the knock while Jennifer was making their snack tray.

"It's the pizza," Jennifer answered the door with excitement.

"You keep avoiding me, and you must have a mentor your first year here." Imani was angry and you could see it on her face.

"I'm in school and I work. When I come home, it's me and my boys. I don't have a lot of time as it is, so I value that. I'm not sure what you want, but I'm private and I don't just share my business with strangers. If I have time tomorrow, I will try then, but right now it's my sons' time and nothing interferes with that." Jennifer was shaking because she'd never stood up for herself like that before. She had no idea what came over her. Jennifer politely closed the door, but soon another knock came. This time, it was the pizza, and movie night was on time.

"Mommy, who is that lady?" Sean asked.

"I don't know," Jennifer shrugged her shoulders and they started with the first movie.

The boys enjoyed movie nights because it was the one night, they could enjoy their favorite soda. Jennifer couldn't shake the look on Imani's face, so she decided to meet with her after Family and Friend's Day was over. Hopefully, it wouldn't be long and drawn out because she rarely got time to herself and she wanted to enjoy what little she had.

"Oh boy, I don't feel like going over there." Jennifer thought to herself. The boys started to fall asleep finally around midnight, so she had them go up to bed while she put up the food. After she cleaned up, she went to bed herself.

Breakfast was simple the next day—a bowl of cereal—but they still watched cartoons together and had a good time being silly. They could hear and see some of the Family and Friends Day activities outside of their window.

People were excited to see their loved ones and they began their days early. Some stayed in the building and others went out after they got their tour. Jennifer smiled and finished the homework she hadn't completed the day before.

"Mommy, somebody's here," the three-year-old came running to his Mom's room shouting.

"Thank you, Isaac, I'll be down in a minute." Jennifer dragged herself to answer the door. "What part of I'll come to you when I am able doesn't this woman understand?" Jennifer was surprised when she opened the door.

"Mom?" Jennifer stepped back to let her mom in followed by her sister, father, and a few others.

"Some lady called telling us she was your mentor, and we should come to this family and friend's thing, so we came. She kept callin' us like it was important. Here we be." Her father thought he was somewhat of a comedian.

"I'll go get dressed and will meet you out there." Jennifer opened the door for them to leave.

"You puttin' us out? We can't see your place?" Her father asked.

"No, I'll see you in a few," Jennifer answered as she escorted them out of her compartment. She was now even more tired of Imani invading her private space. "Okay, guys, we're hanging with our family for a few hours today and then we'll get back to part two of our movie night weekend." The boys were excited about seeing their grandparents and wanted to play with the other kids in the play area.

"Come on, show us around!" They all pulled on Jennifer's arm at one time. Before her coming out, they had been loud and rude to the other people in the Commons, including Imani when she tried to introduce herself.

"I see why she didn't invite them." Imani thought to herself.

"You should've called or said something. We had no idea where you were." Her mom had a way of using guilt trips to make it appear that Jennifer was being distant.

"I told you the day I was moving in." Jennifer's mom gave her a look that said to be quiet.

"Well, you should have called us to remind us." Jennifer and her mom stated together. She figured hearing how often they gave the same excuses would help them see what she was talking about, but it backfired. Her mom slapped her and said she had a smart mouth. Jennifer grabbed her face and walked away. She continued the tour, staying close to her sons and noticing that they knew more about the Commons than she did.

"How did they learn this place so quickly?" Jennifer thought to herself. People seemed to cater to them whenever they went to a restaurant or playground area. Jennifer was uncomfortable with all the attention they were getting, but her family took full advantage as usual.

"We can wait our turn," Jennifer noticed the other people in the restaurant who'd been there long before they got there. "It's not fair to the people who were here first." Jennifer looked around to notice people staring at her. She wanted to disappear so badly it hurt. She turned her focus towards her sons.

Jennifer's family became angry when she turned down the favors and the special treatment. They thought she was being selfish and not thinking about them. Jennifer only wanted to do what was right.

"I have to live here. My sons must live here. Pissing off our neighbors is not a good move. Why don't you see this is not about you?" Jennifer kept her cool. "Of course, how I feel doesn't matter." Jennifer noticed her family wasn't paying attention, so she took the boys and went back to their compartment. When they get there, they notice Imani is blocking their doorway. Jennifer rushes her boys inside.

"Not now, Imani, we'll talk later. This sucky day is your fault." Imani had front row seats to the way her family disrespected and shamed her in front of everyone. They were wanting all the benefits without giving anything. Imani was angered by their actions and if she couldn't talk to Jennifer; she was talking to the family. They may not like what she had to say, but they were going to fix what they broke before they left. Imani had a little over an hour to make her point and arrange an apology, whether real or fake.

"Hello. I came to speak to Jennifer for a moment." Imani demanded. She wanted to see if anyone noticed she'd disappeared. What would be their response? The family pretended to be shocked when they realized Jennifer was nowhere to be found. Imani immediately shut their lies down and told them everything she saw, exposing them for the frauds they were.

"You have less than an hour to make it right, or I promise you that'll be the last time you see her or your grandsons. If you love her the way you say you do, then show her." When Imani was done, Jennifer's family had no choice but to make things right.

As they approached Jennifer's compartment, Imani's words rang in their heads.

"Stop coming and taking from her, leaving her empty. Make her want to invite you back. Whether you like it or not, she can block you. With the way you treated her today, I wouldn't blame her if she did." Imani stood up and walked away. She tried to knock on Jennifer's door. She wanted to console her so badly but couldn't bring herself to knock. She decided to wait until Jennifer came to her.

When Jennifer finally had a chance to check her voicemail, she finally got good news! Her campus housing was ready, and she was ready to leave.

"Things are getting better, finally!" Jennifer walked by the mirror and noticed her face had swollen from where her mom slapped her. She grabbed an ice pack and placed it in a towel to hold on to the swollen area.

Putting the boys to bed was easy, but she had a tough time getting herself calmed down enough to go herself. Jennifer decided to forego church for the day, choosing to watch it online instead. Climbing in the bed, she hears a knock at the door.

"I swear if it's Imani, I'm not ... I just don't have the patience to deal with this right now," Jennifer answered the door and was shocked to see her family. Her mom blushed when she saw the ice pack Jennifer had on her face. She stood in the doorway waiting on them to say something.

"Can we come in?" Jennifer stood firm and didn't move. "We just wanted to apologize for the way things went. I shouldn't have slapped you. I should have taken time to listen to what you were saying." Her mom led the apology and others followed. They all felt hollow and empty to Jennifer, but she accepted it anyway. She wondered why they adopted her if they didn't want her.

She'd known since she was five that she was adopted. Since then, she'd always wondered who her birth family was. She noticed Imani watching from a distance and took one last look at her family.

"The last time." Jennifer thought to herself. "Good night. I have an early day tomorrow. Thanks for coming. You don't have to come back." Jennifer closed the door and locked it. Tears fell from her eyes uncontrollably and she couldn't stop them. She started to call Dr. Polk, but she called Laaek instead. Her best friend knew what to do even when Jennifer was silent on the phone.

Packing her things that night wasn't hard because she hadn't completely unpacked so she would be prepared to move on campus. Laaek managed to leave with Jennifer and the boys the next morning without anyone noticing she'd spent the night. The morning was quiet, but everyone was a bit groggy and tired. It seemed to flow more smoothly than any morning since Jennifer had become a mom.

"Make it a great day!" Jennifer hugged and kissed each of her kids as she dropped them off. She headed to school early to get her room assignment and found out it was a nice apartment. It was everything she'd hoped for and more. It was all overwhelming and she can move in whenever she wanted.

"You need breakfast, and you need to call your doctor." Laaek was in tough love mode. "I know you try to handle things on your own, but you need her help. Don't lose ground now. You've come too far!" Jennifer promised to think about it and then headed back to get the rest of her things from the Commons.

"Jennifer, I waited for you last night, and then you left early this morning. I want to say this one thing and I will go. I requested to be your mentor to protect you from Helen. I hadn't told anyone this but you. From the look of things, I guess you're moving, so I no longer have to do that. I wasn't trying to be in your business nor make you uncomfortable. I wanted you to know I'm here for you and that someone has your back." Jennifer saw the sincerity and somehow found herself wishing they would've talked sooner.

"Excuse me one moment. I need to take this." Jennifer steps away to take the call. The news she received was disturbing. She came back to Imani. "There was a flood in the building where I'm moving to and it'll be at least another three weeks before I can move in. My best friend just took my things to her garage until I could move in. I suppose I owe you a thank you for my family's apology or apologies, whichever it was. Thank you!"

Jennifer's energy was spent, and she had no more will to fight. Imani held her and didn't let her go. She wanted Jennifer to know and see that she wasn't alone. Jennifer melted in her arms, feeling like she was in her mother's arms.

Helen didn't find out that Jennifer had moved in until after Family and Friends Day when her family was the topic of all discussions. She made it her business to show up at Jennifer's door and give her a proper welcome. Jennifer stopped packing and just sat in a chair wondering why things are so hard for her.

"La La, Can the boys hang with you today? I just need a minute to recoup." Laaek was more than happy to have her godsons spend the night. Jennifer decided to write some things down so that she won't be caught off guard again. "Even if I have to stay in a hotel, I've got to get out of here."

* * *

Helen Horrors!

Helen wasn't always mean and bossy. She had a human side that was changed by a story she refused to tell. Helen had a way of celebrating that left her full of regret, but for now, vodka was king and tequila shots were its queen.

"If they could see me now. The bastards! My family don't haf ta come see me. I'm in control now and they can't stop me. I have all this, and they got nuttin' Halers!" Helen was in a drunken stupor, drinking to drown the pain of no one showing up for her during Family and Friends Day. "She's the ugly one, she's so dark, and what happened to her face?" Helen recalled the voices of her past. She promised herself that, when she was grown up, no one would boss her around. "We're identical twins, you assholes."

Helen could barely sit up let alone stand. Her face was swollen from the tears she shed. She looked around her oval office feeling empty and alone. Bailey came to the rescue and drove her home so no one would see her in her weakened state. Bailey hated that he'd have to arrest her one day. He began to understand that she was battling with demons and needed a doctor, not to be arrested.

He didn't understand the compassion he felt for Helen, but even more so he didn't know the secret his mother was keeping from him. Having to pretend he doesn't know who she is was hard, especially when he'd had a rough day with Helen.

Helen had found out the hard way that she and her sister weren't the babies her mom wanted. She still remembered the day she and her sister were removed from the home. She had no idea what happened to her sister, but it felt good not to be in her shadow for once. That was good for her until Jennifer came along. There she was, competing with someone who had her face all over again.

There was nothing Helen could do to appease her family. They saw her as a loser and a troublemaker and let her know that often. As a child, she tried to make things easier for her parents by cleaning and even learning how to cook so her mom wouldn't be so tired. It was never appreciated and someone else always took the credit.

In her teenage years, Helen stopped doing everything and was beaten so badly some days she couldn't move. She was raped at the age of four by her adopted father and, when she tried to tell, the abuse worsened. They both beat her naked for hours. Helen was lost and couldn't figure out what she did wrong. She internalized the abuse for years and then one day realized she didn't have to be the victim. She used the anger to fuel her and became the bully. She fought with herself because it wasn't who she wanted to be, but it's the only way she felt safe and as if no one could hurt her again.

No one believed Helen was abused because her parents had a way of covering it up. They had to keep the checks coming in, so they made things look better than what they were. Helen had to fight at home and school. No matter where she went; she was a target. Eventually, she began attacking first and, that way, people knew to leave her alone.

The only disadvantage was that Helen eventually lost control and couldn't turn it off. Now, even when she didn't want to attack, it became a natural reaction to being triggered that she can no longer fight against.

Jennifer had a long day and stopped by her compartment before going to pick up the boys. She was so tired that she sat down to tie her shoes and fell asleep. A constant tapping awoke her, making her realize someone was knocking on the door.

"Hello," Jennifer's froze in fear. The one person she avoided her entire life was staring at her face to face.

"Hi, girl! How are you?" Jennifer didn't say a word.

"Helen, you know Jennifer?" Imani asked.

"Yeah, we were friends in high school." Jennifer had a confused look on her face. High school must have been a different place or maybe she was thinking of someone else. "I am so sorry I didn't greet you when you moved in, so we are making up for the lost time. Did you enjoy Family and Friends Day? Everyone was nice to you right?" Jennifer nodded.

"It was good." She moved hesitantly, inviting Helen into her compartment.

"I need to show you a few things around the Commons, so follow me. As Jennifer turned to lock the door, Helen grabbed her butt and reminded Jennifer who always had the upper hand.

"She does remember," Jennifer thought to herself. She rolled her eyes and slowly turned around to realize no one saw what she did as usual. She began to follow Helen around the Commons.

"This is your building? I'm assuming." Jennifer tried to keep the conversation going so Helen would focus on talking about herself and not touching her.

"Yes, I thought I would be the helping hand to those in need. It is my pleasure to serve my community as a leader." Helen loved talking about herself and it was the one trick that worked in high school to keep her from touching Jennifer or beating her up.

"I love what you've done with the place. My sons love the play area, and the stores are quite lovely." Jennifer prayed to be able to keep her talking so that she could avoid the horrors of her past. Helen caught on to what she was doing as Jennifer made mention of going to pick up her sons.

"Don't worry, Jen. I am not that same woman. My hand accidentally bumped against you when I clumsily tripped. It won't happen again." Jennifer didn't believe her, but she patronized her to be able to leave unharmed.

"It's forgiven. I need to go pick up my kids from school. Nice seeing you again." Jennifer ran to the car and let out a scream once she was in her car. "WHY?" Jennifer drove off to avoid sitting in the car crying. She never would've made it to get her boys.

"Don't come in here lying to me," Laaek demanded.

"I had a great day! How are you?" Jennifer sarcastically responded.

"Mommy was crying." Sean pointed out.

"Tattletale." Jennifer stuck her tongue at her son and smiled. It was her way of letting him know everything was okay.

"You're going to talk to me today and you're not leaving until you do. Number two, we are calling Dr. Polk! She said I was free to do that when you were being stubborn. Number three, I don't know what happened, but some of your clothes are here and you are spending the night so we can finish this discussion. These are not suggestions nor are they requests. It's mandatory!" Jennifer noticed her boys were listening very closely and didn't put up a fight.

"I'm fine. I just got a little overwhelmed with the on-campus housing thing and some classwork things, but I can turn that in by Friday and I'm okay... really." Jennifer looked up to notice that Laaek's face said NON-NEGOTIABLE.

"Where are you guys going?" Sam came to grab his Mom's hand.

"Godmee's taking us to play at Chuck E Cheese's and then we're going to Legoland and a movie." Jennifer smiled.

"Wow, that sounds like fun. I can just go..." Jennifer started but her best friend's face didn't change. "I'll take a nap and you guys enjoy. Bring me some snacks and a t-shirt please!" Jennifer went to her room and settled in. She grabbed her journal to write in it because she knew that'd be the first thing Dr. Polk would ask about and she hadn't started at all. "No sense in being in trouble by everybody." Jennifer thought to herself. "Ain't nobody scared of her." Jennifer began to write.

"I heard that!" Laaek shouted as she and the boys walked out the door.

"I'm talkin' to myself," Jennifer responded. Her nap was interrupted by continuous nightmares of the abuse she suffered at the hands of Helen. She'd even heard some of the other ladies complaining about how she sexually, physically, and verbally abused them. She was the same horror she'd always been and now she was stronger and much worse.

"Please leave me alone! I haven't done anything to you." Jennifer pleaded.

"You think you're better than me and prettier than me! I wear this face better than you ever could." Helen shouted and she shoved Jennifer's head into the toilet and flushed it. When someone walked in, she pretended to be helping Jennifer. She claimed that something she ate made her stomach sick. Jennifer knew better and went along with it. Waking in a cold sweat, Jennifer found herself calling Imani.

"Hi... I'm sorry to bother you. but I thought... I thought..." Jennifer didn't know what to say.

"Hello. You are not a bother. Are you okay?" Imani was hoping this would get her to open up and talk.

"Yeah, I was just letting you know that it'll be too late for us to come back, so we're staying at my best friend's house. I'm sorry. I don't know what I was thinking. I'll let you get back to what you were doing." Jennifer nervously tried to hang up when she heard something that made her burst into tears.

"I saw what she did to you." Imani paused. "Helen has been terrorizing the women in this place and a few of the men too. No one dares to stand up to her and, until you are willing to fight, no one can fight for you." Jennifer remained silent. She desperately wanted to get off the phone but didn't want to be rude.

"So, you are telling me it is okay for her to grab you the way she did? You're okay with that?" Imani was met with more silence. She could hear Jennifer sobbing heavily over the phone.

"I'm not going anywhere. I will wait and, when you are ready, we can talk." Imani waited patiently for Jennifer to gather herself.

"I need to go. I have schoolwork to finish and I'm somewhat behind and I need to fix dinner so everyone can eat when they come back. Thanks again for listening." Jennifer quickly hung up the phone before she started crying again. She buried her head under the covers and didn't move again until her sons came in the door. They brought her Zaxby's, her favorite, and a cold cherry Pepsi. It was just what the doctor ordered.

"Okay, guys, let's get a bath and pajamas on while Mommy eats." The boys followed their godmother and began to get ready for bed.

"You and I are going to get on the phone with Dr. Polk once I get them down. Enjoy!" Laaek was not letting it go, so Jennifer enjoyed her food while she awaited the dreadful conversation she was going to have with the Doctor.

"She's going to know I haven't done anything she told me to do. I wasn't going back for the next session. I think I've missed a few. This is going to be interesting." Jennifer thought to herself. "She is not answering her phone, so we will call her the first thing in the morning on the way to school." Laaek went into her room and closed the door. Jennifer kissed her boys goodnight and, to her surprise, was able to fall asleep.

Nightmares tortured Jennifer most of the evening and, one time, she woke everyone up because she screamed so loudly. Laaek tried but couldn't wake her up and had to get the boys to go back to sleep.

"She'll be fine, she probably is dreaming about winning the lottery or something." Laaek tried waking Jennifer up one more time.

"You're having a nightmare. Let's pray so we can all get some sleep. They both prayed together, and Jennifer slept peacefully until it was time to get up.

The next morning Jennifer woke up to a phone call she wished she could've avoided.

"You need to see me immediately or we are going to talk to your boss. I've documented every date missed so far. Now, have you completed the entries in the journal as I've asked you to?" Jennifer was silent. "I didn't think so. You need to come to see me, and we can talk further." Jennifer's face was red with embarrassment and fear. She was in big trouble and not sure how to handle it. For Laaek, however, it was hilarious, and she laughed the entire time Jennifer squirmed on the phone.

"I told you so." Laaek dropped Jennifer off at the doctor's office and was her chauffer for the day so Jennifer wouldn't run away.

"I hate you sometimes." Jennifer blurted out.

"I love you too sweetie, tell me how it goes. I've got class." Laaek blew her bestie a kiss and went to class.

"Jennifer, in here." Dr. Polk was firm and not leaving room for backing out. Jennifer kept trying to tell her legs to run, but the signal was lost, and she ended up walking into the office with Dr. Polk. "Let me see your journal." Dr. Polk held out her hand. Jennifer tried to explain, but she was not moved by her sad face or excuses. She just stood with her hand held out. Shamefully, Jennifer handed her the journal with only a half entry inside. "There's nothing in here. Except for something you started and didn't finish." Frustration was written all over Dr. Polk's face, but she managed to maintain her cool. "Here's what we're going to do. I'm going to end the session here and we are going to sit and speak with your boss." Jennifer just nodded her head. She didn't know what else to do as she aimlessly followed Dr. Polk to her boss's office.

"I am so fired." Jennifer thought to herself. Dr. Polk went in to talk to her colleague first.

"I came to inform you that the student you referred to me has missed three appointments and, when I asked for her journal, I received a half entry. I can't help her if she won't do the work! I'll do anything for you, John, but I won't force her if she's not ready." Dr. Harris stepped out of his office and gave Jennifer a stern look. Tears fell from her face as she tried to muster up an apology, but nothing would come out.

"In my office, young lady." Jennifer slowly walks into the office where she is double teamed and placed on a final warning. The way they spoke to her, she would've preferred a spanking instead. "Miss one more appointment and you'll wish we never met." Dr. Harris was in full father mode and Jennifer knew not to rebut.

"Yes sir!" Jennifer agreed.

"Now, you owe my colleague a sincere apology, and I want nothing but progress this day forward." Jennifer turned to Dr. Polk and apologized.

"Here's your journal. I want you to complete the assignment I gave you to write your daily thought and, on top of that, I want you to write the following affirmations one thousand times. Say them out loud and yes record them because right now I don't trust you." Trembling, Jennifer takes her journal and accepts her assignments.

"I can't believe this. I have other stuff to do, and I have kids and uuugghhh!" Jennifer mumbles as she walks out the door.

"Jennifer, you have something you'd like to say?" Dr. Polk asked with a smile on her face.

"No ma'am... just organizing to myself out loud. She was scared to look in Dr. Harris's direction but could feel his glare on the side of her face. "I've got class in a few, so I'll just take this and go." Jennifer couldn't get out of there fast enough. What was she to write about? Her life was embarrassing, and Helen was only one of the reasons.

CHAPTER THREE

Revelation

"Here's a pillow so you can have a comfortable ride home."
—Laaek

"Mommy, we had so much fun at godmee's house and we played with friends at Chuck E Cheese's, too. We went to a museum and learned stuff like at school." Sam was never this talkative, but he had a lot to say this time. Then Sean and Isaac chimed in as well. It sounded like the only one who had a rough, butt chewing kind of day was her.

"Great! I'm glad you enjoyed yourselves. Let's grab our things and get ready to go. We've got lots of packing to do because we're moving soon, and I have a ton of homework." Jennifer could hear Laaek laughing in the back.

"Boys, here are your snacks to go and you and I will talk later. I got an earful from both Dr. Harris and Dr. Polk. No more escaping and running, ma'am. I even packed you a snack to go as well. I heard how rough your day was. Here's a pillow so you can have a comfortable ride home." Laaek laughed some more.

"You know it's because I love you and I don't want to see you fall apart." Jennifer rolled her eyes as she walked out the door and placed her kids in the car. The pillow turned out to be a true comfort after the conversation she had with both doctors. She decided to have a fun day with her sons before she got started to help ease the tension of the day.

"Hello," Jennifer answered quickly when she saw who it was.

"I couldn't say this in the office, but if you miss another appointment, I have a purse with a detachable strap. I'll let you interpret that any way you need to. Have a good one." Jennifer's face dropped.

"Guys, we can only do one thing tonight because mom's got tons to do. I will make it up to you when I'm done. Is that cool?" The boys had fallen asleep in the car, so they heard nothing. She woke everyone up so they could walk inside and took all their snacks and placed them on the table.

"Hello. May I speak to Imani please?" Imani had answered the phone.

"This is she." Jennifer took a deep breath.

"Would you mind coming over? I need help with something, and I am not sure how to do it. If you're busy, I understand." Imani agreed to come and was there in less than five minutes. "I have snacks and something to drink if you're hungry. It's just until I cook dinner." Imani grabbed Jennifer's hands.

"Calm your spirit, it'll be okay. We can talk when you're ready. I'm not going anywhere until you ask me to." Jennifer took a deep breath.

"Once they are done with their snacks, we do their homework then I do mine. They are only able to play games or watch TV after they have read one book. I ask them questions, and, on Fridays, we do a play of their favorite story. Once they are done with their homework and book, I will be able to talk because they will be watching their show. I'll give them headsets so I can talk freely. In the meantime, if you want, you can join us for snacks or have a seat in the living room... the TV is free." Imani agreed to have snacks with them, and she turned out to be fun to get along with. She was great with the boys. When Jennifer had the boys situated with their movie, she joined Imani on the couch.

"You're a good mother. I am proud of the way you are raising them." Imani listened and waited with patience.

"I don't know where to start. Helen and I met in high school and she tortured me every day. If it wasn't sexual abuse, it was physical. If not that, verbal and sometimes all the above. She has a way of making herself look like the victim and no one ever believed she would ever hurt me. She was so popular, and I wasn't. I was told that I was looking for attention and making things up. I wasn't the only one she hurt, but the others were afraid to speak up, so I stopped talking about it eventually and just dealt with it. At home, I was sexually abused by my adopted father hence my three sons. I have never had a boyfriend nor been in love. I am just trying to make things happen for them, so they never have to know the monsters I grew up with. It gets overwhelming for me and I have panic attacks, so I have to see a therapist now and I have all this work to do, but I'm not sure where to start. I can lose everything if I don't do them, and I have worked too hard to get where I am. I just can't face those demons in my past without falling apart. I need help." Imani listened intently and was more than happy to help Jennifer with her issue. She tried to convince her to report Helen, but that was a hard no.

"Helen always gets away and the best thing for me to do is to get away from her. I'm moving at the end of the month." Imani saw Jennifer shaking with fear and didn't push the issue any further.

"I know one day you'll have the strength you need to fight. You're going to have to get her to stop. You overcome the bully by confronting the bully and not by running away. I will help you the best way I can, but without you or your testimony, there's not much I can do." Jennifer understood and made plans to avoid being at the Commons until it was time for bed.

"Excuse me. One moment." Imani stepped outside to take a call. "Bailey, is everything okay?" Imani asked.

"Yes, Mom. I am fine, but Helen is getting worse. More women are complaining about how she's treating them, and we are ready to make an arrest. The companies in the Commons are saying she's not paying as she promised and she's defrauding the residents by stealing their money. She's coming up with contracts so that they have to give her full control over their lives. Don't sign anything over to her and don't give her access to anything of yours or ours." Bailey explained in detail what he saw and prepared his Mom for the worst. Imani went back inside, wanting to say something, but couldn't bring herself to utter the words that were deep in her soul, so she waited.

"I'm your mother," Imani whispered as she returned home.

Jennifer decided to eat at the Commons that day. She had no idea what came over her, but she didn't have the energy to leave. She looked at her phone to see what time it was when a call came in.

"Hi, Mom! Our friend is having a birthday party. It's Kameron and Kalaab. Can we spend the night? Godmee said she'll take us if you say yes. Does Isaac have to come with us? He always gets in the way." Sam was on a roll and didn't take a breath until he finished talking. Laaek took the phone and took over the call.

"The boys wanted to go to their friend's house for a party and they don't want their little brother to go. He and I can hang out if you're okay with them going to the party." Laaek laughed at Sam's honesty.

"Yeah, that's not a problem. I know their mom very well. Where's their little brother going? Usually, Isaac hangs with Isaiah." Laaek thought about it.

"I don't know, but I can call and ask her if you want." Jennifer gave her the number so she could reach the mom and get the info.

"Alright. Give me fifteen minutes and I'll call you back. Jennifer placed the order for her food before she got another call.

"Hi. I'm not disturbing you, am I?" Jennifer looked up and a young girl about her age was standing at her table. Jennifer was shocked.

"No. How can I help?" MacKenzy sat down across from her.

"I am new here and I don't know anyone. Everyone seems to be so much older than me and there's a nice older lady I met. Imani, I think. I just am trying to figure things out." MacKenzy looked around and Jennifer could see the fear on her face.

"I am Jennifer and I'm pretty new too. I can try to help as best I can." Just then, the phone rang.

"Okay. I talked to the mom, Genisha, and she said that Isaiah can hang with me and the boys can hang with her." Laaek was good at handling details.

"Thanks, sis! My food is on the way out, so I'll talk to you when I'm done eating." Jennifer returned her focus to MacKenzy.

"Where are you from?" MacKenzy fidgeted.

"After my mom had to go to the hospital, I was tossed from foster home to foster home. I'm still in high school and I graduate next year. I just didn't want to stay in another foster home, so I came here. I know I shouldn't have lied about my age, but they wouldn't take me unless I was eighteen." MacKenzy kept looking around the restaurant.

"Have you eaten yet?" Jennifer asked. MacKenzy got quiet. Jennifer called the server over and added to her order so that she and MacKenzy could share.

"Don't worry. It's going to be okay." Jennifer wanted to make MacKenzy feel comfortable and unafraid.

"Did anybody tell you that you look like that lady that runs this place?" Jennifer sighed.

"Yes," she responded out loud. "Unfortunately," she responded to herself. "I get that a lot, but I guess everyone has a twin somewhere. How are you doing in school?"

"I'm in college. I graduated at an early age which no one thought I could do." Jennifer found that it was easy to talk to MacKenzy and it felt good to encourage her to finish school and not give up. They had an amazing conversation and Jennifer promised to keep in touch. She wasn't too eager to tell her that she was moving but did mention her door would always be open.

Jennifer headed back to her compartment to catch up on assignments and study for some upcoming tests. She had an appointment with Dr. Polk that she didn't want to miss, so she thought she would get a head start.

"This is going to be a long day." Jennifer thought to herself. Once she got in her compartment, she felt uneasy but had to shake it off. She only had five hours before her appointment, and she didn't want any mishaps.

"Laaek, do me a favor and call me at 1 pm to make sure I'm up and on my way to my appointment. I want to get there by 1:30 that way, if I fall asleep, I'm in the office." Laaek laughed as she agreed.

"You don't want to miss any more appointments. I'm likin' this lady more and more every day." Jennifer huffed.

"Shut up and just call me please." Jennifer wasn't in the mood for her sarcasm.

"I got you, sis!" Laaek continued to laugh.

"May I speak with my bear?" Laaek handed Isaac the phone. "Hi, my precious one, how are you?" Isaac just held the phone and smiled.

"Talk baby," Laaek encouraged.

"Hi, Mommy! Isaiah is here and we're going to play at the jump place where you can jump. Godmee got us some toys and we're going to play with them. I got coloring books, too, and I'm going to make you a picture." Isaac talked for at least ten minutes straight.

"I'm so happy for you. Mommy is going to do homework and then I have a meeting. When I am done, may I come play with you?" Isaac laughed.

"Yes, Mommy, I'll play with you. Isaiah too!" Isaac handed Laaek the phone and Jennifer returned to doing her work. She seemed distracted but couldn't figure out why her attention was all over the place. Restless, she figured maybe she'd take a nap and get back to it once she rested a little. Several hours later, Jennifer woke up to a knock at the door.

"I am on my way out, so whoever that is will have to wait until I get back. I can't believe I slept that long. I am just glad I woke up on time. Ask people to call and they don't, but she has two small people, so she probably forgot." When Jennifer opened the door, she was surprised.

"Dr. Polk I was just on our way to our appointment. I didn't know you made house calls." Dr. Polk seemed agitated.

"I don't... only when my clients miss a second appointment and don't call to tell you they're not coming." Jennifer looked at her phone and saw it was nearly 4 pm.

"Oh my gosh, I am so sorry! I had no idea that I missed it. I fell asleep and I was supposed to get a call to wake me up." She further looked to see she missed several calls from Laaek. "I missed the calls, the alarm, everything." Jennifer knew her fate and it wasn't looking good.

When the session was over, Jennifer was ready to quit. She remembered all the advice she'd given MacKenzy and thought it was a load of crap. She remembered the promise she made her son, so she went to go see him. He always made her days happier along with his brothers.

"I can't believe she was serious about that strap on her purse." Jennifer slowly got in the car and had to get herself together so she could play with her boy and his bestie.

"I want to do some finger painting. We are going to get good and messy." Jennifer's plan worked. She and her bestie had a good messy time with the boys.

"What happened to you? You started working out or something? Why are you walking like that?" Jennifer looked at Laaek with frustration on her face and pain on her backside.

"Leave me alone okay. I have had a long hard day and I just want to have fun with my small people." There was no way Jennifer was going to tell Laaek what happened. She'd never live it down. Jennifer managed to sit next to her son and hide the pain she was in.

"What do we do first?" Isaiah handed her a smock to wear and some paints.

"We are going to paint something we do outside." Jennifer thought for a moment.

"What about a picnic?" Isaiah smiled.

"Okay! You can do a picnic and we're going to do football." Isaac was ready to go. "Isaac, what part are you painting?" Isaac grabbed the brown paint.

"I'm painting a football!" They all had a good time and were covered in paint by the end of the day. Once the kids were down, Jennifer went to take a bath before she left.

"You don't take baths. You're going to tell me what's up." Laaek went back to the kitchen to grab a cup of tea to relax. Jennifer rolled her eyes and continued to get cleaned up.

On the way back to the Commons, she felt a new sense of hope when she realized she only had one week to go before she would move into her on-campus housing. A smile came over her face as she was so excited to get away from that horrid place.

Helen used her master key to sneak into residents' compartments and take what she wanted. Many of the women who'd been abused began to report her to the police and this was making Bailey's and Jackson's investigation easier. It was about to come to an end and Helen would be made responsible for everything she'd done from fraud to sexual assault. It wouldn't be long before they could bring her in.

"Come to bed Imani. Why are you worried?" Imani looked at her husband.

"I'm not sure how to tell the family about my girls. I have no idea where to start. They will never forgive me. I was a monster to them and now Helen is who I used to be, and Jennifer is trying hard to fight not to be. I've made a mess and I don't know how to clean it up." Abel grabbed his wife's hand and looked into her eyes.

"You have done what you know how to survive. Trust God to open the door when the time is right. Then, trust God with what happens afterward. You have two amazing sons that you raised well. One is a cop and one on his way to college. That means you learned from your mistakes. It will get better… just be patient." Imani agreed and joined her husband. She couldn't stop wondering if she'd see Jennifer again or what would end up happening to Helen. Her thoughts raced the entire night.

"God, help me tell my daughters the truth and their brother, too. I need your help! In Jesus' name Amen." Imani closed her eyes, but sleep wouldn't find her until about 3 am.

On the other side of the building, Jennifer was about to be awakened by her worst nightmare.

"Close your mouth! If you make a sound, I will kill you." Jennifer couldn't tell if it was a dream or not.

"What… what's going on?" Groggy Jennifer tried to get up but found herself being forced back down onto the bed. Jennifer fights again and is knocked down again. A moment of clarity shows her that this is real. She immediately tries to get up so she can grab her boys and run. Then she remembers they're not there and she fights to free herself.

"Bitch, I said stay down!" At that moment, she recognized the voice, and everything came back. It's Helen and she's the same monster she was when they were in high school.

"Helen, please don't do this. Stop!" Jennifer pleaded, but she knew it wouldn't work. Helen came for what she wanted and nothing else mattered. MacKenzy walked by and saw what was happening. She called for help.

* * *

"Justice"

"Hi. I'm looking for Jennifer. I'm dropping off her boys today." Imani didn't know what to say. She just stood still.

"Hello. I went by her place and I didn't get an answer. That's not like her." Laaek was growing impatient.

"She has been taken to the hospital. There was an accident." Laaek waited for more information.

"Do I have to ask where or are you going to tell me what's going on?" Imani was fidgety and didn't know what to say.

"Hi, ma'am. I'm officer Bailey and Jennifer was attacked along with another young lady. They were both taken to the hospital. Is it possible the boys can stay with you until her release?" Laaek was floored and could barely compose herself.

"What hospital? Attacked? What happened? Isn't this place supposed to be secure? She suddenly remembered she had the boys with her and calmed down. She could tell they were afraid, and she wasn't making things any better.

"She's at Franklin Memorial and so far, everything's looking good." Imani wanted to say something, but she couldn't. She couldn't believe what she saw and didn't know how to respond. Abel came to find his wife in a daze and escorted her back to their compartment.

"You did well. I know it was hard for you to do, but you did the right thing." Imani was still in shock from finding Jennifer and MacKenzy raped and nearly beaten to death.

Laaek made a mad dash for the hospital and stopped by Genisha's to see if the boys could stay there while she went to check on their mom. She was more than willing to keep the boys and wanted updates on Jennifer's progress.

On the way to the hospital, Laaek took deep breaths and listened to some music to calm her spirit. In her mind, when she found out what happened, whoever was responsible was going to pay. She was ready to cut off body parts if she had to. Praying was the furthest thing from her mind though she tried to pull it in closer to pray for her friend who'd become a sister. In the meantime, the residents were worried about what was going to happen now.

"Ladies and gentlemen, we understand you are concerned about your living arrangements. Please know that the city will not close the place down and will do its best to find a replacement as we have taken over the building. Unfortunately, the former owner has not handled things properly including being arrested for sexual assault and battery. We need to know if anyone else has been attacked by Miss Helen White? If you would please come forward, it would greatly help the investigation. We also want you to know that your money will be given back to you as soon as we can get the books closed.

Please allow us the time we need to investigate and fully refund you. We apologize for any inconvenience and thank you for your patience. In the meantime, you are welcome to stay, and we will stand watch to make sure things flow smoothly."

Jackson could see the fear on their faces and wasn't sure how to comfort them. He was still in the middle of trying to resolve his issues; however, he had a duty to the innocent people who were misused by a power-hungry woman.

Laaek arrived at the hospital in no time. "I'm looking for Jennifer Collins please." The nurse looked in her directory and pointed towards the room where Jennifer was. Hesitantly, Laaek walked into the room and saw her friend bandaged up.

"Hi, the boys are fine and with Genisha. She asked me to call and let her know you're okay." Jennifer laid silently not wanting to talk or say anything. "I called Dr. Polk, and she's on her way. I figured she could handle this better than me. Maybe she could help me." Laaek began to feel as if she were talking to herself, so she sat down and waited.

"Hi ladies, I came as fast as I could, and..." Dr. Polk was stopped in her tracks. "What happened?" Laaek shrugged her shoulders.

"I'm not sure, she hasn't spoken yet. I don't know if it's shock or anger or both. I'm waiting to find out myself." Dr. Polk knew exactly what to do to get Jennifer to talk.

"Hello. I got a call from Laaek and she's concerned about you. I know this is difficult and probably a major setback for you, but we have learned that being silent doesn't bring the healing you need." Dr. Polk sat on the bed next to Jennifer and held her hand. "I want to show you some people who need you to get well." Dr. Polk pulled out her phone and showed her a picture she'd taken. In the picture were Jennifer and her sons. "These four people need you to show up for them and be strong for them. You've come so far, and I don't want you to turn back because of this. It doesn't define you." Dr. Polk was patient and waited. Jennifer looked at the picture and began to talk.

"Where's MacKenzy?" Everyone was confused.

"Who's MacKenzy?" Laaek asked. Jennifer went silent again.

"I applaud your effort but try a little harder. Look at your sons and come back to them. If you want them to be safe and not get hurt, then you need to talk. Let's try again." Jennifer turned her head and was looking at Dr. Polk eye to eye.

"WHY? WHY DOES SHE GET AWAY WITH THIS? WHY DOES SHE GET TO DO THIS OVER AND OVER AGAIN? WHY CAN'T ANYONE SEE HER FOR THE TRASH SHE IS? WHY CAN SHE HURT PEOPLE AND NO ONE SAY OR DO ANYTHING? WHY?" Jennifer burst into tears and Dr. Polk held her in her arms.

"Those questions are valid, but most important right now is knowing what happened, so she doesn't get away with it again. I'm here for and with you and your best friend is here with you. You have to fight because we can't do it for you." Jennifer calmed a little. Tears were streaming down her face.

"I was asleep and woke up to see Helen on top of me. I tried to fight her off but kept blacking out. When I woke up, she was having sex with me and I was tied to the bed. The more I resisted, the more she beat me, but I couldn't see with what. In my mind, I left. I couldn't physically escape, but I was not worried about my sons they were with their Godmee and I just left. I hoped she wouldn't kill me. I heard screams for help or something but that's all I remember." Jennifer had a solemn look on her face as if she didn't want to cry anymore. She was tired and embarrassed and done. How did she let this happen again? She had always been so careful and couldn't believe that she let her guard down.

"Is MacKenzy okay? She's a new girl and I promise I thought I heard her screaming for help. I don't know if it was before or after Helen broke in, but I heard her... I think." Dr. Polk and Laaek were confused. Laaek was in tears, she couldn't believe that something so horrid happened to her best friend.

"NO," Jennifer could see what was on her bestie's mind and stopped her before she could formulate a plan. "You will NOT do anything to anyone. I'm okay! I've gotten over this before and

I'll do it again. You are NOT going to jail. NO!" Jennifer started to cry again, and her best friend embraced her as they cried together.

Dr. Polk went to get the officers that were on the case and Jennifer was able to tell them what happened to her. Dr. Polk smiled with pride as she held her hand to support her as she told her story.

"Unfortunately, you and MacKenzy weren't the only ones she assaulted. Now that you are coming forward, the others will come forward as well. You are brave!" Jackson and Bailey verified that they had everything they needed, and they left.

"Officer? How's MacKenzy?" Bailey fought back tears.

"She's doing fine. She was trying to come to see you to get help, but she heard what Helen was doing to you, so she called out as much as she could until someone called us." Jackson tapped his partner on the shoulder to let him know it was time to go.

"Thank you!" Jennifer smiled.

"I am so proud of you. You got through the hardest part and now you don't ever have to deal with this from her again." Dr. Polk reached over and hugged Jennifer as if she were hugging her own. Something about the hug brought back memories of a young child she had as a patient.

They had a relationship to this day and she often told Imani about Jennifer not realizing their connection. "Okay, so get well and I will see you once you are healed physically and then we can get you whole on the inside." Dr. Polk gave a kiss to her forehead and wished her well as she left.

"I called Genisha, and she wants you to call when you're ready. She wants to know you're okay. The boys are doing great and have lots of questions, but she's managed to divert their attention to other things. They know you so well." Jennifer smiled as she thought of her sons.

"I'm so embarrassed." Jennifer placed her hands over her face. "I should've seen this coming. I should've known better." Laaek sat next to her friend.

"This is not on you! You did everything you could to move and none of this is on you. Even if you did have to stay there, it's still not your fault. She violated your trust. She broke into your place and took advantage of her authority over you." Laaek felt the rage rising in her all over again. "We are going to get through this together. I got you!" Laaek laid next to her best friend and they talked until Jennifer fell asleep. It was time to go when the nurses began to come in and check on Jennifer.

Laaek left and picked up the boys. Genisha volunteered to tag along and all of them went to the park to let the boys play.

"What do you need?" Genisha asked. "I know we are not familiar with each other, but I consider Jennifer to be a good friend. Our kids have grown up together and I'm surprised we've not met before. I want you to know that I understand this is hard to deal with and you are not by yourself." Laaek never thought about her feelings. She was so concerned about Jennifer, she forgot about her own.

"Thank you, right now I'm so angry I could kill her. I know it's not what I'm supposed to be thinking but she's been doing this for a long time. We grew up together and went to different schools. She would always try to get help, but no one believed her. Now I wish I would've done… Never mind. I just want her to pay for what she's done. Jennifer has been through so much and she keeps rising no matter what. She doesn't deserve this." Laaek shed a few tears. It felt good to have someone to talk to in the way she'd been there for Jennifer.

"Maybe you should also look into counseling. Though you weren't in her shoes, it seems that whatever Jennifer went through, you went through, too." Genisha had a point and it made sense. Maybe that was why she was so adamant about Jennifer getting help. Getting counseling for herself wasn't something she thought about until now. It could probably be the thing that helped control her rage. Laaek thought about it and figured if she thought any longer, she'd talk herself out of it.

"Hello," Laaek stepped to the side and pulled out her phone. "Hello, this is Laaek, can we talk?"

"It's a few weeks before the trial and I've checked on the ladies in the hospital and the ladies at the Commons. Everyone is on edge. We're going to need protection for them in case she has some form of retaliation. You never know who she's working with if anyone." Bailey tried to recall if he saw anyone strange, but he didn't remember anyone. Helen was private and she made sure that what she didn't want anyone else to know was well hidden.

"I think I found her," Jackson stated. "You sure? How do you know?" Jackson shrugged.

"I don't. I just have a gut feeling about it. I'm waiting for some results now and I'll know for sure. Right now, I want to throw the entire book at that woman for what she's done to these people." Jackson had a look of rage that made Helen's attacks seem personal.

"You okay?" Jackson nodded his head. "Let's get this paperwork together—this bitch is goin' down!" Jackson walked off as if he were on a vengeance. Bailey wasn't sure what it was about, but he realized it got serious just that fast.

The air in the city of Atlanta was growing thick around the Commons and Bailey was concerned for his partner and friend. Many felt like Helen would get away with things as usual. Confidence in the legal system was at an all-time low for those who were poor. The rich could do anything they wanted and get away with it. The residents had to admit that things were running a lot more smoothly with Helen behind bars.

The locks were changed, and the people were able to freely live their lives. It's the way it should have been when the doors opened.

"I've got to talk to my daughter." Imani looked at her husband. "When I return, we will tell the boys about their sisters and hopefully things will be okay. I can no longer keep this secret inside of me." Imani grabbed her things and headed towards the jail. Abel shook his head and hoped for the best. He knew once his wife was determined to do something, there was no stopping her. He didn't think the family was necessarily ready to hear the whole truth, but he supported her in that she needed to do something.

"God, go with my wife on her truth journey. She's going to need You." Abel returned to his work.

MacKenzy and Jennifer were released on the same day. Jennifer was able to check on her and made herself available any time she needed to talk. Laaek showed up not too long afterward and helped Jennifer move on campus. The housing was ready early due to the college finding out about her incident. They even gave her an upgrade to help her move into a safer environment. Jennifer made sure to give MacKenzy her address and phone number. She didn't want her to feel as if she was alone. She even gave her Dr. Polk's card so that she could get help dealing with her emotions. This was the first time anything like this had happened to her, though she did have some trauma as a child. It was more physical and neglect, but never sexual abuse.

"Thank you, I thought I was going to be here alone." Jennifer hugged MacKenzy.

"You've got me, Imani seems nice, and a few others. We're all here for you. I consider you to be a little sister." Jennifer offered to treat MacKenzy to lunch before she left.

"I'd love to go eat at the one restaurant on the corner. I think it's Mexican." Jennifer laughed.

"It's Mexican and, yes, we can go there." The two walked together to enjoy a "see you later" celebration in honor of Jennifer getting her place on campus.

"You know, when you graduate, you should consider college. There are great opportunities that are waiting for you and you don't have to wait on anyone else to be great. You can be great because it's what you want to be." MacKenzy smiled. No one ever told her she could be great before nor did they care.

"I would like to go to college." Jennifer smiled. "One moment please." Jennifer stepped away to take a phone call.

"Hello." MacKenzy looked up to see who was speaking to her. She recognized the voice but didn't remember who it was until she saw him.

"Officer Jackson, right?" Jackson sat down.

"Yes, it's me. I just wanted to check in with you and see how you were doing." MacKenzy was grateful that an officer would check up on her.

"I'm okay! We're just about to eat some lunch before Jennifer moves." Jackson was quiet.

"I think I'm your father." MacKenzy fainted and Jackson caught her.

CHAPTER FOUR

The Trial

"He said he might be my father. Someone I'd never met before. It was always just me and my mother."—MacKenzy

"Jennifer, I'm sorry to call so late. I had a nightmare, and I can't sleep. I know she's not here, but I can't help feeling she's going to come through that door any minute now." MacKenzy was shaking so hard it was in her voice.

"Okay. I'll be there in a minute. Can you pack a bag? You can come spend the night here if you'd like." Jennifer couldn't sleep herself.

"Are you okay? I was going to call my therapist, but this is too late in the evening. We can help each other tonight, how does that sound?" MacKenzy was all for it.

"Do you remember Jackson?" Jennifer thought for a moment.

"Yeah, you scared me when you fainted. What did he say to you?" MacKezny tried to hold back the tears.

"He said he might be my father. Someone I'd never met before. It was always just me and my mother. She's in the mental hospital because she had a breakdown. No one ever told me what was going on with her. They always said I was too young to understand. I ran away and that's how I ended up here. I thought she was going to send me back and now I wish she would have. This was the worst and it made being home not so bad at all." MacKenzy was still shaking, so Jennifer made her some tea and held her for a while until she felt comfortable. In Jennifer's mind, this was her little sister and she had to look out for her.

"I'm not sure what to say, but I'm sure my doctor can help you. Did you ever call her?" MacKenzy was embarrassed.

"Not yet, I just don't have money like that, and I didn't want to bother her.

"The police department is paying for it because of the incident, so you don't have to worry about that. They'll take care of the appointments for as long as you need them. I get mine through school and my professor/boss is good friends with her. He makes sure I get what I need. He's like a father to me, so I'm grateful for all he's taught me. Would you like to see where you'll be sleeping?" MacKenzy grabbed her things and went upstairs to see the room where'd she'd be. Jennifer laid out some pajamas for her and some personal items such as soap and deodorants along with things for her to take a nice bath.

"Hopefully, this will help you get relaxed. I'm going back to bed because the boys and I have an early day. You've got school tomorrow, so get some rest. You are still going." MacKenzy smiled.

"You're like a mom." Jennifer smiled back.

"I am a mom, but we'll talk about that another time. Good night!" Jennifer went to check on her boys and, on the way back to her room, she stopped by to make sure MacKenzy was good to go.

Once she went back to her room, she felt good herself. She was able to get to sleep. Somehow having MacKenzy near her made her feel as if she could protect her and keep her safe. Jennifer had a habit of looking out for everyone else but herself.

First thing the next morning, they took time to talk to Dr. Polk, and she helped them to navigate through the anxiety. The trial was days away and they knew they had to confront the one woman who'd made their days miserable.

"Jennifer, come see me!" Dr. Harris called Jennifer into his office. "I just wanted to check on you and see how you were doing. You can have days off work if you need them and get healthy. I understand." Jennifer never saw him flustered before. He was always so strong, demanding, and sure. This was the first time he seemed afraid and not in control. He grabbed her and hugged her. With tears falling from his face, he let her know he was there for her. "I know I'm not your father, but to me, you're my daughter. I never want anything to hurt you. I push you because I know you're great. I'm so sorry I wasn't there to protect you from this bully. I wish I could've been there for you from the day you were born. I would've loved being your protector, your guide, your friend, your father." Dr. Harris held her a little while longer to let her know that she was his little girl.

Jennifer never knew how much he cared until that moment. She felt safe and protected for the first time in her life. She melted and allowed him to love her as the father she needed to have right then.

"Thank you, sir! I'm okay to work for now and if I need anything, I'll let you know." Jennifer returned to classes feeling loved and comforted. "Somebody loves me," Jennifer whispered to herself. She smiled and walked to class with a pep in her step.

The Commons Part One

Jackson sat in his office with papers in his hand that confirmed his suspicions. He'd finally found his daughter and wanted to be in her life. He'd been searching for years and had a hard time because his wife disappeared before she was born. He struggled with being able to find other missing kids but not his own.

"Hey bruh, you okay?" Jackson looked up.

"Bailey, I'm great! Come in and close the door." Bailey grabbed a seat. "I found her. MacKenzy's my daughter. It took me 17 years to find her, and I missed her entire life. I'm going to be there for her now. That woman is not getting away with what she's done to her nor the other women. I'm going to make sure of it!" Bailey was concerned because the look on his partner's face was frightening.

"Maybe you're too close and you should back off this one. Let us take care of it." Jackson looked at Bailey.

"I have every right to be here. I had no idea I'd find my girl, but I'm not going to let that interfere in the same way it didn't interfere when this investigation began. Keep your mouth shut. You're more than a partner. You're my best friend. I trust you with my life. I got this." Jackson stood up and slammed some paperwork on the desk.

"Damn!" Bailey agreed to keep it to himself.

"I'm here for you, bro, but you need to talk to somebody or somethn'. You're slippin'. Don't lose this case because of a personal endeavor. Let's do this by the book so this woman can go to jail and pay for her crimes." Jackson knew Bailey was right, but he was stubborn. He could handle things on his own and didn't need anyone's help. Bailey began to pray for his friend and hoped that he'd get the help he needed before it all exploded in his face.

"You ladies will be prepped for court so that the questions and the process won't overwhelm you. Please don't be frightened and just tell the truth. We want to make sure she pays for what she's done to you. She has a host of charges which include fraud and tax evasion. These charges added will guarantee she stays in jail a long time." Jackson continued to explain.

CHAPTER FIVE

Confessions

"I am your mother and Jennifer is your twin sister."
—Imani

"Helen, you have a visitor." The guard opened her cell and began to walk her towards the visitor's room. She had no idea who'd be visiting her, but she assumed that it was her lawyer. When she saw Imani, her flesh cringed.

"What do you want? You here to gloat and say I told you so? You here to pray and throw scriptures at me? What you here to make me yo' bitch now? What do you want? Helen ranted in anger. Imani didn't respond, partly because she didn't know how to say what she needed to say. Imani regained her composure from her silent rage and focused on Helen eye to eye.

"I am your mother, and Jennifer is your twin sister." Helen was stopped in the middle of her raging tantrum. She stared at Imani as images began to resurface about her childhood. Helen's face carried the expression of one who'd just seen a ghost from their past.

"You… you're the reason why I'm like this. You made my life hell! GUARD!" Helen couldn't get away from Imani fast enough. Imani felt as if she failed again. She had no clue how to fix what she'd broken.

"There's no way they'd forgive me now." Imani left more defeated than when she came. She was determined not to give up. She just needed a way to make things right. She's regretted who she was to her girls and hated the day they were taken from her. It seemed she lost everything at once and she had to get it back.

"Hello, old friend, I need your help. I finally opened up to the girls and told them the truth. I saw you at the park and you were speaking to another young lady. I didn't want to disturb you. I know at our last meeting I was avoiding the issue and I've only made things worse. I'm ready to listen. Please help me get my family back. Once you get this message, call me." Imani had to swallow her pride and give in to what Dr. Polk had been telling her for years.

She'd hidden in fear for so long, she wasn't sure she could cope with the strength of the truth. It felt as if its power were overwhelming and would sweep her under its authority. That frightened her but losing her family frightened her more.

Imani grabbed a notebook and began writing down everything she wanted to happen from the smallest things to the biggest things. The more she wrote, the more energized she was to do what it took to get her family together.

"Imani, I got your message. I have one question for you. Are you seriously ready because you say yes, then you run when things get tough? I want you to take some time to think about what you're asking me to do." Dr. Polk knew what she was in for but wanted to give Imani the chance to prove herself.

"I am desperate," Imani could barely talk because the fear of the future nearly took her breath away. "I will do it. I won't run this time. I just need a way to make sure my family is whole and healed and we're together. I want to break this curse off my family for good." Dr. Polk was silent.

"We'll see!" Dr. Polk responded as she hung up the phone. She was concerned that this time would be like previous times when Imani attempted to change and would disappear when Dr. Polk challenged the most difficult areas in her life.

"Oh boy, we're in for a long haul with this one." Imani sighed.

"Let me guess, Imani." Rico knew when his wife was stressed about Imani. She only had that certain facial expression for this one person who seemed to wear and tear on her the most. Maybe it was because she's known Imani since Imani was a child.

"Don't worry, she'll get it. I like the fact that she keeps trying." Rico kissed his wife on the forehead and went to watch TV. "Come watch wrestling with me. Relax, take your mind off things." Dr. Polk agreed. It wasn't hard especially when she looked to see her favorite assortment of cookies and snacks on the TV table.

"God, I need your help. I want to make this work this time." Imani slowly walked towards her couch to sit down.

"MacKenzy," Jackson called as she was speedily walking past him. MacKenzy pretended not to hear him at first, but then curiosity got the better of her.

"Yes, how can I help you?" MacKenzy said, not slowing down much.

"I know what you heard was shocking." Jackson reached out and grabbed her arm and released her when she jumped back in fear. "I'm not trying to hurt you. I just want to get to know you. I've been looking for you and your mother ever since she disappeared. I went to work one day and came home and you both were gone. I never knew what happened." Jackson was near tears.

MacKenzy began to listen to what he was saying. It did make better sense to her than what her mother had always told her about her father.

"She's in the hospital. She has mental issues, and I was placed in a foster home. I was better off with her." Jackson always knew there was something wrong with his wife, but she wouldn't get the help she needed. It was the one thing they fought about constantly.

He listened intently to what she was saying and wished he could change the last seventeen or so years of her life. Feeling hopeless, Jackson reaches out to his daughter hoping she would allow him to be the father he was robbed of being. He didn't want her to have negative feelings about her mom but, from what he heard; she'd done a good enough job of that all on her own.

"We've got lots of catching up to do. There's a lot you don't know, and I will tell you when it's time. Right now, I just want some time to get to know you." MacKenzy had to admit in all her pain, she always wanted to know where her dad was. Now she had the opportunity to know him the way she'd always dreamed about.

"We can do that." MacKenzy was afraid, yet she wanted to know the man she never got to see—the one she daydreamed about every day of her life. Is this her knight in shining armor? She can finally be in a stable home, finish school, and do all the things she'd longed to do as a little girl. She couldn't wait to tell Jennifer about how she and her dad had plans and that she could finally leave the Commons. Her stomach was filled with butterflies and she had to admit that, despite the fear, she felt a sense of hope. MacKenzy took Jackson to meet Jennifer. She didn't want to go alone just in case he was a crazy stalker.

"Hello. I'm Jackson. Nice to meet you." Jennifer shook his hand while mean-mugging him right in the eye.

"I remember you. Nice to meet you as well. I never got to thank you for helping us during the trial. I'm glad you were able to find your daughter. By the way, how did you know it was MacKenzy?" Jennifer never changed the look on her face.

"Getting' right down to the nitty-gritty, I see. I'd been looking for her since her mom disappeared. She was seven months pregnant at the time. I came home from work one day and everything was gone. She'd changed her name several times and I thought MacKenzy would be in a foster home but wasn't able to find her there. They told me she ran away. Being a cop, I found out what her name was because I had access to her doctor's records. I tried everything and to find her now is just a blessing. I don't want to waste any time getting to know her and love her like the princess she is." Jennifer liked what he said, but she didn't let him see it.

"How are you girls feeling now that Helen is behind bars for the rest of her life? If it's not a good time, I understand. I'll do my best to keep protecting you all from any of her backlash rage." The girls looked at each other.

"We're okay and, so far, we've been there for each other. Plus, my friends have been there for us." Jennifer took on the protective role for MacKenzy. She was determined never to let anyone hurt her again. She'd been protective of kids ever since she was a kid herself.

"I'm paying the bill today so everyone can get what they want." Jackson was in the best mood. He'd found his daughter, and nothing could put a damper on his mood. They all enjoyed their day out and got to know Jackson a little better. He wasn't so bad.

The families at the Commons were all properly placed in safe homes where Helen couldn't find them. Jackson and Bailey made sure that they were secure. The road was still long in their fight to make sure Helen didn't escape the justice system the way she had so many times before. Her rap sheet was so long that people thought it was a scroll from the early 1800s.

"Bailey, are you sure you want to dig up your past?" Bailey gathered his thoughts.

"I want to know the truth about what happened. There has to be more to the story than what I got. I can't just accept it was an accident." Bailey grabbed his picture and kissed it. Jackson knew how he felt especially when he thought his daughter died. He knew this had to be rough not to know what happened to his favorite people in the world.

The tables were turning, and it was time for him to win. He had to admit that, deep down inside, he was afraid of what he'd find out. Jackson was concerned, too, because he had a hunch as to who the culprit was.

"Alright, we'll get started first thing in the morning. I promised you I would, and I want to be there for you. Thanks for sacrificing yourself to help me." Jackson and Bailey agreed to meet in the morning.

"Jennifer, just confirming our appointment for tomorrow. I'll see you then." Jennifer was glad she decided to listen to her messages. She was going to sleep in and nearly forgot about the appointment.

"I wonder when I'll be able to stop seeing her." Jennifer thought to herself.

"I know you're tired of seeing me, but we're making progress and we need to keep it going. Don't roll your eyes at me either. See you tomorrow." Jennifer looked at her phone to see if her camera was on.

"She has to have a camera somewhere around here and I'm going to find it." Jennifer put her phone on the charger and joined her boys for some good ole fashioned cartoons and cookies.

"Mommy, you think we can go to Disney World one day and see Mickey Mouse and Goofy?" Sam asked.

"Yeah, I want to ride the rides and play there, too." Sean chimed in.

"I like Mickey Mouse," Isaac added. Jennifer looked her boys in the eyes and couldn't resist.

"Sure, we can go. We'll start planning for it as soon as I have a summer vacation from school and Dr. Polk," she mumbled the Dr. Polk part.

"Mommy, you know the doctor is good for you. You have to take your medicine so you can feel better." Isaac shocked Jennifer. She had no idea he knew so much.

"You're right, my sweet pea. The doctor is good for me." Jennifer made a note to watch what she mumbled around him in the future. "Seriously guys, I have to be out of school, so I don't have to worry about studying, classes, work, or appointments. It won't take me long, I promise." The boys understood and they went back to watching cartoons.

* * *

"The Finding"

Jackson and Bailey got busy and began collecting evidence that seemed to be overlooked. Bailey went back to his old neighborhood. Memories of good time flooded his brain. He remembered the good days as if they were happening at that moment.

"What you thinkin' about?" Bailey shrugged his shoulders.

"Any little thing helps you know." Jackson was trying to help him talk about it that way it may trigger a clue to help them find the information they were looking for.

"I know. I'm hoping against hope but where are their bodies? How do people just disappear? They can't be dead." Bailey became frustrated when he suddenly remembered a place that they never told anyone about.

"Bailey, where are you going?" Bailey's pace grew faster, and he was moving so quickly Jackson had to run to keep up. "Bailey, STOP!" Just then, they came up on what appeared to be an abandoned shed in the back of his old yard. It was made to look unappealing on the outside so no one would expect anyone to be in it. Inside, it was safe enough to be a bomb shed.

"It's been a year and I know it's hard. I'm sorry, brother, but you may have to face the fact that they're not here anymore. That place is not livable." Bailey opened the first door and behind that door was another door. The passcode was still the same. A familiar aroma came across their noses.

"Daddy!" Bailey dropped to his knees in tears. He couldn't believe what he was seeing and looked to Jackson to see if it were real. Coming up behind his little girl were his son and his wife.

"We knew to come here and hide. We waited for you and weren't sure if you'd been killed or what was going on. I knew you'd find us." Bailey stood to give his wife a passionate kiss and hugged everyone.

Jackson was amazed by what he saw. He had to know what happened but didn't want to disturb the family reunion. He was so relieved for his friend.

"We still need to find out who did this and we need to make sure they never do it again". That moment was overwhelming, so they agreed to talk about it the next morning. Bailey just wanted to be with his family and Jackson understood.

www.ingramcontent.com/pod-product-compliance
Lightning Source LLC
Chambersburg PA
CBHW060334260626
47160CB00007B/2793